Veronica Mueller

Jessica

Veronica
Linn
mueller

Veronica

Linn

Mueller

Weekly Reader Books presents

THUNDERHOOF

Story and Pictures by
SYD HOFF

An EARLY I CAN READ Book

Harper & Row, Publishers
New York, Evanston, San Francisco, London

This book is a presentation of Weekly Reader Books.
Weekly Reader Books offers book clubs for children from
preschool through junior high school.

For further information write to:
Weekly Reader Books
1250 Fairwood Ave.
Columbus, Ohio 43216

THUNDERHOOF

Copyright © 1971 by Syd Hoff

Trade Standard Book Number 06-022559-9
Harpercrest Standard Book Number 06-022560-2

Library of Congress Catalog Card Number: 75-129855

I Can Read Book is a registered trademark of Harper & Row,
Publishers, Inc.

*For my father,
who refused to let me
become a cowboy.*

Way out West,

one great horse still ran wild.

His name was Thunderhoof.

5

Cowboys tried to catch him.

But he ran too fast for them.

If they got a rope around his neck,

he shook it off.

"Nobody will ever catch me,"

said Thunderhoof.

And he went on running

across the open range.

Every night

he slept under the blue sky.

One day,

when Thunderhoof woke up,

he found the rivers dry.

There was no water left to drink.

11

He got so weak he could not run.

He got so weak he could hardly walk.

When a rope landed on his neck,

he could not shake it off.

"Come with us," said some cowboys.

They took Thunderhoof back

to the ranch.

They gave him water.

They gave him hay.

They brushed him.

They rubbed his nose.

They took the burrs out of his mane

and said,

"Nice horse, nice old feller."

Then they put a saddle on Thunderhoof
and tried to ride him.

Off went one cowboy.

Off went another cowboy.

Nobody could stay on Thunderhoof
very long.

"It is no use keeping that horse,"

said the ranch owner.

"We might as well turn him loose."

They took the saddle off Thunderhoof

and let him go.

Thunderhoof went back

to the open range.

Once more he ran wild.

Once more he slept under the blue sky.

It rained,

and there was water to drink.

But Thunderhoof was not happy.

27

He missed having someone brush him,

rub his nose,

take the burrs out of his mane,

and say,

"Nice horse, nice old feller."

28

Thunderhoof went back to the ranch.

He let them put on that saddle.

This time

he let the cowboys ride him.

"I think I will stay here,"

said Thunderhoof.

"I think I will stay for good."

31

And he did.